Tadpoles

Dad's Cake

Crabtree Publishing Company
www.crabtreebooks.com
1-800-387-7650

PMB 16A, 350 Fifth Ave.
Suite 3308,
New York, NY

616 Welland Ave.
St. Catharines, ON
L2M 5V6

Published by Crabtree Publishing in 2010

Series Editor: Jackie Hamley
Editor: Reagan Miller
Series Advisor: Dr. Hilary Minns
Series Designer: Peter Scoulding
Editorial Director: Kathy Middleton

Text © Margaret Nash 2008
Illustration © Jane Cope 2008

The rights of the author and the illustrator
of this Work have been asserted.

First published in 2008
by Franklin Watts
(A division of Hachette
Children's Books)

**Library and Archives Canada
Cataloguing in Publication**

Nash, Margaret, 1939-
      Dad's cake / Margaret Nash ; illustrated by
Jane Cope.

(Tadpoles)
ISBN 978-0-7787-3865-7 (bound).--
ISBN 978-0-7787-3896-1 (pbk.)

      1. Readers (Primary). 2. Readers--Cake.
3. Readers--Fathers and sons. I. Cope, Jane
II. Title. III. Series: Tadpoles (St. Catharines, Ont.)

PE1117.T33 2009   428.6   C2009-903983-4

**Library of Congress
Cataloging-in-Publication Data**

Nash, Margaret, 1939-
 Dad's cake / by Margaret Nash ; illustrated by
Jane Cope.
      p. cm. -- (Tadpoles)
 Summary: Dad asks Jed to help him make a cake
with strange ingredients which keeps Jed guessing
as to who this cake is for.
 ISBN 978-0-7787-3896-1 (pbk. : alk. paper) -- ISBN
978-0-7787-3865-7 (reinforced lib. bdg. : alk. paper)
[1. Fathers and sons--Fiction. 2. Baking--Fiction.
3. Cake--Fiction. 4. Humorous stories.] I. Cope,
Jane, ill. II. Title. III. Series.

PZ7.N1732Dc 2009
[E]--dc22

                                    2009025291

Dad's Cake

by Margaret Nash

Illustrated by Jane Cope

Crabtree Publishing Company

www.crabtreebooks.com

Margaret Nash

"Cakes are yummy! My son once made one in a very small tin. When it came out of the oven it was almost as tall as a chimney!"

Jane Cope

"I love making cakes, although eating them is the best bit! Unless it's a cake like the one Dad is making ..."

"Let's make a cake,"
said Dad.

"Who for?" said Jed.

"Ah!" said Dad.

"You will see!"

Dad gave Jed a
bowl and a very
big spoon, then ...

9

... a bit of this,

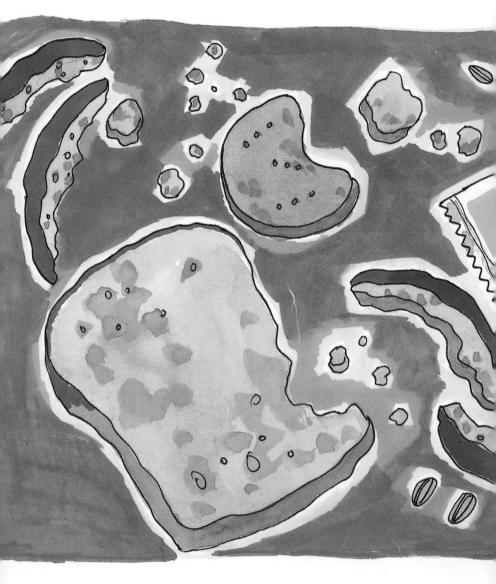

and a lot of these ...

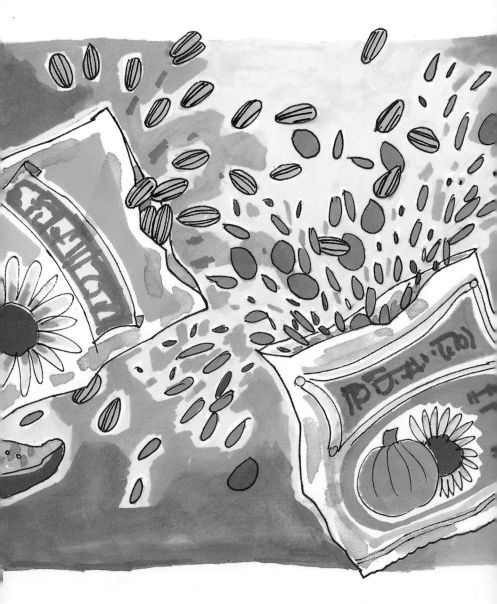

... scraps of fat,

and lumps of cheese.

"Yuck!" said Jed.
"Who will want
this cake?"

15

"Not me!" said Dad.
"But someone will!"

17

"But Dad, **nobody** will want this cake!" said Jed.

"Ah!" said Dad.
"They will! You will
see!"

And they did!

Notes for adults

TADPOLES are structured to provide support for early readers. The stories may also be used by adults for sharing with young children.

Starting to read alone can be daunting. **TADPOLES** help by providing visual support and repeating high frequency words and phrases. These books will both develop confidence and encourage reading and rereading for pleasure.

If you are reading this book with a child, here are a few suggestions:

1. Make reading fun! Choose a time to read when you and the child are relaxed and have time to share the story.
2. Talk about the story before you start reading. Look at the cover and the blurb. What might the story be about? Why might the child like it?
3. Encourage the child to reread the story, and to retell the story in their own words, using the illustrations to remind them what has happened.
4. Discuss the story and see if the child can relate it to their own experiences, or perhaps compare it to another story they know.
5. Give praise! Children learn best in a positive environment.

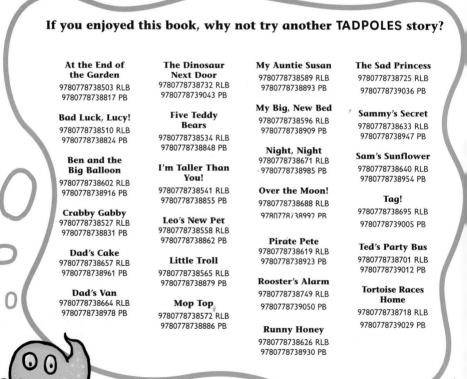

If you enjoyed this book, why not try another TADPOLES story?